MT. P

Dear Parent:

Congratulations! Your child is taking the first steps on an exciting journey. The destination? Independent reading!

STEP INTO READING® will help your child get there. The program offers five steps to reading success. Each step includes fun stories and colorful art. There are also Step into Reading Sticker Books, Step into Reading Math Readers, Step into Reading Phonics Readers, Step into Reading Write-In Readers, and Step into Reading Phonics Boxed Sets—a complete literacy program with something to interest every child.

Learning to Read, Step by Step!

Ready to Read   Preschool–Kindergarten
• big type and easy words • rhyme and rhythm • picture clues
For children who know the alphabet and are eager to begin reading.

Reading with Help   Preschool–Grade 1
• basic vocabulary • short sentences • simple stories
For children who recognize familiar words and sound out new words with help.

Reading on Your Own   Grades 1–3
• engaging characters • easy-to-follow plots • popular topics
For children who are ready to read on their own.

Reading Paragraphs   Grades 2–3
• challenging vocabulary • short paragraphs • exciting stories
For newly independent readers who read simple sentences with confidence.

Ready for Chapters   Grades 2–4
• chapters • longer paragraphs • full-color art
For children who want to take the plunge into chapter books but still like colorful pictures.

STEP INTO READING® is designed to give every child a successful reading experience. The grade levels are only guides. Children can progress through the steps at their own speed, developing confidence in their reading, no matter what their grade.

Remember, a lifetime love of reading starts with a single step!

Visit us on the Web!
StepIntoReading.com
randomhouse.com/kids
www.pocoyo.com

Educators and librarians, for a variety of teaching tools, visit us at
randomhouse.com/teachers

ISBN 978-0-307-98099-1 (trade) — ISBN 978-0-375-97134-1 (lib. bdg.)

Printed in the United States of America   10 9 8 7 6 5 4 3 2 1

POCOYO™

Surprise for Pocoyo

By Christy Webster

Random House 🏠 New York

This is Pocoyo.

These are his friends.

Pato is a duck.

Elly is an elephant.

Loula is a dog.

Sleepy Bird is a bird.

Pocoyo's friends
want to surprise him.

Here comes Pocoyo.

His friends are gone!

Pato and Sleepy Bird
make a cake.
They have eggs
and milk.

Pocoyo is coming!

Pato hides
in an egg.
Sleepy Bird hides
under a bowl.

Pocoyo sees eggs.

Pocoyo sees milk.

Pocoyo goes
to find his friends.

Pocoyo is gone.

Pato and Sleepy Bird

come out.

Pocoyo did not see them!

Elly and Loula

blow up balloons.

Pocoyo is coming!

Loula hides.

Elly hides
by a tree.
Pocoyo does not
see her.

21

It is almost time
for the surprise.

Loula brings balloons.
Pato brings cake.

Pocoyo cannot find
his friends.
He is sad.

They are right
behind him!

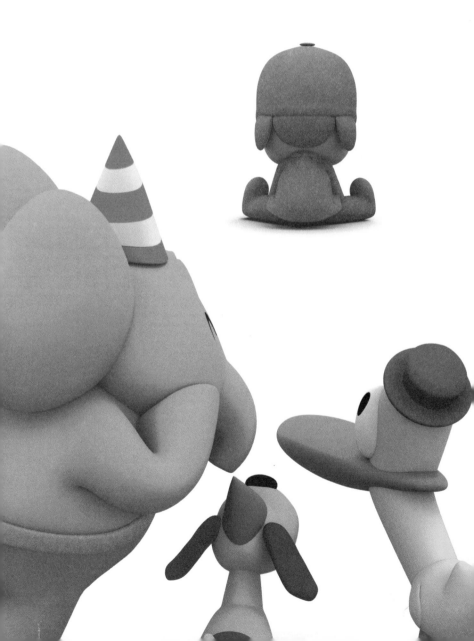

Surprise!
It is a party!

There is cake.

There are balloons.

There are hats.

Everyone dances.

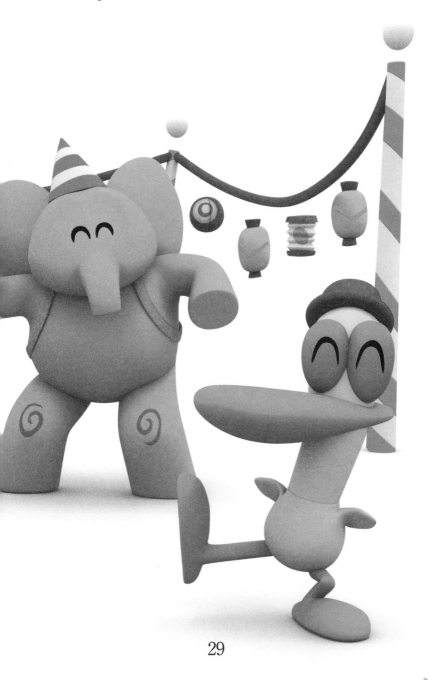

Hooray for Pocoyo!

Hooray for surprises!

Hooray for friends!